BRIGID'S JOURNEY
TO THE WORLD'S EDGE
A folktale in the Irish Tradition

By Harry Michael Bagdasian

Adapted from the play
JOURNEY TO THE WORLD'S EDGE
Scripted by Harry M. Bagdasian & Ernest Joselovitz
Originally commissioned by IMAGINATION STAGE, Bethesda, MD
Acting edition available from Dramatic Publishing, Inc.

Write Directions, LLC
11425 Fairoak Drive
Silver Spring, MD 20902
240-381-3196

BRIGID'S JOURNEY TO THE WORLD'S EDGE

THE PLAY, Journey to the World's Edge, was originally commissioned and premiered by Imagination Stage of Washington, DC. As written by Harry Michael Bagdasian and Ernest Joselovitz. It has been performed over 100 times by schools, churches and theatre groups in nineteen different states in the United States and several times in Canada.

Cover & Title page illustration courtesy of Imagination Stage.

First published in paperback by Write Directions, LLC January 2018

copyright ©MMXVIII by
HARRY MICHAEL BAGDASIAN
Library of Congress Control Number: 2018900835
ISBN 9780999256138

Author's Representative
Maryann Karinch, The Rudy Agency
825 Wildlife Lane
Estes Park, CO   80517
maryann@karinch.com

ADDITIONAL WORKS BY
Harry M. Bagdasian

CAUTION: Spider in baggie in freezer
A (short) Comic Novel about Finding Resolvel in Middle Age
And Courage in The Middle Ages

YA Novels
BRIGID'S JOURNEY TO THE WORLD'S EDGE

PLAY ANTHOLOGIES
COMEDY FOR LOTS OF GIRLS
And some guys

"SOMETIMES YA JUST GOTT MAKE YOUR PLAY"
Five short plays for young actors

PLAYS
HeHEE! Or "What? It's Not Glee?"
With Liam Brennan

CARRYING ON
A one-act comedy published by Dramatic Publishing

Ten Anthololgies of Comedy Sketches For Young Performers
By Harry M. Bagdasian – some in collaboration with Lisa Itte' and others
Information at www.ContemporaryDrama.Com

4 Plays for Young Audiences with Ernie Joselovitz
CAPTURE THE MOON
Large and small cast editions
JOURNEY TO THE WORLD'S EDGE
RIDDLE ME A PRINCE
With music by Lenny Williams and lyrics by Bari Biern

More At www.hbagdasian.org

TABLE OF CONTENTS

INTRODUCTION

WHAT YOU MIGHT WANT TO KNOW AS WE BEGIN

Before I tell you the story of Brigid Shawn O'Grady of long-ago County Clare, Ireland, I believe it is best that you know she succeeds in her adventure. Yes, right here at the top of this tale, you should know that she will reach the well at the world's edge. She also encounters the wise old woman that the mythic Sea Mither describes to Brigid when the powerful sea goddess first appears to her at the Cliffs of Moher.

Have I good reason to reveal such facts at the beginning of this tale? I believe I do. I can't help but think that one day you will read this story to younger folk. There's no need to be frightening them unnecessarily as Brigid confronts several scary creatures and dangerous situations before she completes her journey.

Have I revealed too much? Fear not. The end of Brigid's journey is not the end of her quest.

CHAPTER ONE
Why Did She Leave The House?

Do you believe in magic? I do and so did Brigid Shawn O'Grady because it is magic that changed things for her many many years ago in County Clare, Ireland. To begin with, Brigid received two important things when she was born: a wonderful book of magical tales from her grandfather and a horribly misshaped foot by a quirk of nature. Her one foot was as normal as can be, but the other was large and looked like a big boot even without the special leather footwear her father crafted for her.

One morning, young Brigid Shawn O'Grady sat by the window of their small farmhouse reading out loud from her book of magical stories.

"Paddy jumped up on the back of the giant sea tern and they rode the west wind to the east which took him closer and closer to the Cliffs of Moher and to his home. The wind suddenly ..."

"Brigid!" Her mother's voice shattered the world of make believe and returned her attention to the real world and to the broom her mother was offering.

"Your reading's lovely, lass, but the floor is not swept and there's wood to fetch!"

The sound of a passing horse drew Brigid to the window where she watched a farmer driving his wagon loaded with hay, and nearby she saw a little girl her own age carrying a book and a lunch pail.

Brigid didn't say anything, but she easily remembered the first time she saw the little girl a couple years before. She was sitting gazing out the window as she was mending clothes with her mother, she saw that little girl for the third time that week.

"That little girl passing our home, that little girl carrying those books, where is she going?" Brigid asked her Mother.

"School," her mother told her.

At the time, "school" was a new word for her.

The memory quickly faded as once again her mother called to her. "Brigid! Please stop your daydreaming."

Brigid turned to her mother. "He's driving his hay

to the village and that girl is going to school in the village. I want to go! I want to see the village."

Brigid's mother handed her the broom. "This floor will not sweep itself."

Brigid took the broom and once again began her morning chores, and once again as she worked, she tried to imagine what "the village" was like and what the little girl was learning in her school. *Is her teacher kind and encouraging like my mother when she teaches me here in our home? What is her home like? Is it like our home?*

Brigid finished with her sweeping and then went out to the yard to fetch water from the well to help with her cleaning.

The O'Grady home was a very comfortable thatched roof cottage with thick walls of peat cut from the bog, a long ways away. The stone fireplace served the family well for preparing meals and for warmth. Surrounding the house were acres of farmland for growing potatoes and wheat and several modest wooden structures. The barn was just big enough for the cow and the plow horse and a winter's supply of grain and straw. The chicken coop and pen for the laying hens was nearby, as was a shed for keeping the tools and the rest of the harvest. Not too far from the cottage were a well that provided fresh water and a small vegetable garden which Brigid tended with great loving care.

Brigid was the only child of a Michael O'Grady and his wife, Mary. Her parents loved her very much despite the fact that she was born with that terribly misshapen foot.

From the day she was born, the people of the nearby village heard of the deformity and imagined her difference signified the most horrible of things. Even without seeing the child, many simply decided that she must be evil. Simply put, the poor child scared just about everyone one except her parents. They loved their daughter very much and did all they could to protect her. They kept her at home and never took her to town or to any public gathering.

As time passed, her misshapen foot did not improve. It caused her to walk with a pronounced limp and it required a special home-made leather boot. By the time she was ten, the special boot looked like a large brown hoof with random stitching crossing this way and that.

Despite this deformity, Brigid was very helpful to her mother and father. She swept the wooden floor of their cottage, drew water from the well behind the house, helped with the washing, the cooking and with tending their vegetable garden. She became quite skillful at keeping her father's axe sharpened and she even learned to split the much-needed firewood. The chopping and the digging in the garden helped Brigid to become unusually strong for a girl her age. Of course, not being able to leave their yard and being kept confined to the cottage during most of the daylight hours, Brigid had no comparison to make with others her age.

Being restricted to such a small part of the world, Brigid became more and more curious about the rest of the world outside her home. Not that much was visible to her. She watched out the little windows of her family's cottage and wondered at the limited sights she could see from her vegetable garden in the side yard.

Day after day she would see the little girl, a girl not

taller than herself and probably the same age she would guess.

"I want to go to school," she insisted one day to her father.

"It is best you stay at home," her Father told her.

Perhaps I didn't ask him properly, Brigid thought, so several days later she asked, "Father, I would like to go to school. May I please?"

Her father took both of her little hands into his big rough hands, looked at her lovingly with his soft blue eyes and told her, "we keep you here at home for your own good."

"You're different, Brigid," her mother added.

"I am?" she asked.

"It is best you stay inside our house," her father gently instructed and let go of her hands.

"Here at home you are safe," her mother assured her.

"There is no need for you to go to the village school. Our home - this is your school. You learn from your mother. She does a good job teaching you numbers and words, does she not?"

"Yes, father, she does."

"You're becoming quite smart, Brigid Shawn O'Grady. Tonight, after supper, would you read to me another tale from your book?"

"Certainly!"

"That's a good girl." He gave her a quick hug, she kissed him on the cheek and then he was out the door, out to the fields to tend the crops.

Brigid loved learning and she loved her leather-bound collection of Irish folk tales that her grandfather had given her when she was born. Her mother taught her to read using that book of dreamy stories and far-away adventures. As Brigid learned her letters and then words, she would read the book of folk tales over and over until the pages were worn.

For the next couple years, Brigid was content to stay in the house, learning from her mother and father and occasionally working in her little vegetable garden next to their cottage. Of course, she was not allowed to stay outside for too long.

Day after day Brigid would see a little girl pass the O'Grady cottage on her way to what she only knew as "the school in the village."

I know what a "village" is. Brigid would think. *But is it like the villages and towns in my book? Is there a castle? Does it have a moat? Is there a marketplace?*

Two more years went by. Brigid grew up inside her world of four walls and a window, reading her one book of tales and legends. She found great comfort in the words of the stories such as, "... and all were happy. So, the Sea Mither smiled, and disappeared again into the ocean waves."

Brigid would read and dream.

However, as time passed, she grew restless, thinking always, *what is a real school like? What is that village like? Is there a princess living in a big castle? Is there a blacksmith shop like in the story about the little boy and his magic steed?"*

Then, all in one day, she saw several different people passing on the road that ran close to the front door of their cottage. There was a very tall bearded man leading his horse as it pulled a cart full of colorful cloth and silks heading to the village. Then there was a farmer and his wife walking from the village with a large basket full of breads and cabbages.

I've never grown a cabbage that large, Brigid thought.

A shepherd with a bundle of sheep's wool tied to his horse was headed to the village followed closely by a young boy leading a horse that had obviously thrown a shoe. The boy stopped and spoke with Brigid's mother who was tending the front walk.

"Good day to you, ma'am."

"To you as well," she answered.

"The man there, the shepherd, he tells me there's a good smithy in the next village. Would he be tellin' truth?"

"Aye. We've an excellent blacksmith, quite the expert with horses, he is."

"Ah, that's good news. Thank you," he said with a smile and a doff of his hat. He then continued down the road towards the village.

Her mother turned and saw Brigid peering out the window and gave a wave.

Brigid waved back and then she retreated to her stool by the hearth and added wood to the small fire under the kettle. As she stirred the fire with the iron poker, she wondered out loud, "A school? A village? There are colorful silks in the village, and woolens and baked bread and school books and maybe more. What else is there? 'Tis a place of mysteries and wonder! I must see for myself what the little girl sees every day."

She had made up her mind.

The next morning, before the sun had risen, when everything was gray and oh-so-still, and her mother and father still asleep, she carefully opened the big front door, stepped out of the cottage and quietly closed the door behind her.

She looked up and then down the road. Not a soul was in sight.

For the first time in her walking, talking life she left the house and yard that had confined her for a little more than fourteen years.

She walked the dirt road she'd never been allowed and was soon on the street in the little village of Lisdoonvarna. There she saw the village green on which she'd never walked, and beyond it, between two very tall pine trees, the wooden schoolhouse of which she had only heard tell.

Suddenly a rooster crowed in the distance. Brigid startled. A shiver ran up her spine to her neck making the hair on the back of her neck bristle.

The sun will soon light the village, she thought. *I should hurry.*

She hurried across the green to the schoolhouse. There she peeked in through the schoolhouse windows and saw the rows of wooden chairs, desks with their ink wells, books and a world of maps upon the walls.

How, she wondered, *could a place so wonderful harm me?*

The aroma of fresh baking bread drew her toward the bake shop where she gazed through the window at soda bread and yesterday's dainty cakes.

Onward Brigid went. At the tailor's shop she was

16

dazzled by the bright red dress and the feathered hats in the store window.

She was distracted by so many wonders that before she knew it, the sun was up and the day had begun. The street cleaner was inspecting his domain. The tailor and the baker were opening their shops. The teacher was opening the school.

Brigid was fascinated by everything she saw as the villagers began their new day. She just stood and stared. Soon there were dozens of people in the street and they crowded together discussing the presence of "that O'Grady child."

The little girl Brigid had seen so often passing her cottage stepped from the crowd and approached Brigid.

"Hi. My name is Brianna. What's your name?"

Brigid wanted to reply. She wanted to be friendly. But the nasty looks from all of the grownups made her want to flee.

Excuse me, I need be going home," Brigid managed to stutter.

"Would you like to play with me?" Brianna asked

her.

The little girl's mother rushed over and planted herself between her daughter and Brigid. "Brianna, keep your distance, little one! Can't you see ... IT?"

"What?" Brigid asked.

"That!" Brianna's mother said with disdain as she pointed to the strangely shaped boot covering Brigid's misshaped foot.

"Ooh, ooh!" Brianna exclaimed and reached to touch Brigid's foot while asking, "Does it hurt?"

"Enough!" Her mother exclaimed as she pulled her daughter away from Brigid. "She's that infant that's grown up now. The one with that ugly foot!"

"My foot?" Brigid asked.

By this time, quite a few people had gathered near her, but they all turned their backs on Brigid. They refused to talk to her, but they certainly had plenty to say to each other about her.

"That affliction! Her frightening difference," said one man to another.

"She's got a hoof, like a sheep, one man told the

woman who ran the clothing store.

'Tis not my fault, ma'am," Brigid tried to tell her, but the woman would not turn 'round and face Brigid.

"Poor thing. She's so twisted on the outside," observed one woman.

"Perhaps the inside as well," her companion replied.

'Tis nothing I've done," Brigid tried to explain to the people who had turned their backs on her.

"That foot! What a frightening mistake."

"She's impossible to clothe properly. With that foot, she's not pretty at all."

"A monster!" decried the street cleaner. He spit on the ground by Brigid's feet causing her to step back. He quickly swept the ground where she once stood.

The villagers continued their comments revealing their fears and hatred for the child who was "different."

"She's not normal."

"She's ugly."

"She doesn't belong!"

"What have I done?" Brigid begged.

They ignored her.

"Do you see her?" another asked.

"I don't."

"I choose not to."

"Me as well."

"Why won't you look at me?" Brigid asked.

The grownups would only look at each other as their comments became louder.

"Someone that ugly."

"A child that strange."

"She should go away!"

"She should disappear like she's never been here!"

"I wish I could," replied Brigid, tears welling up in her eyes.

"I don't see her."

"I never saw her."

"Me neither."

"Stop ... stop ... stop!" Brigid pleaded, backing away from the mob. Her misshaped foot stepped on a stone, not a really big one, but big enough for her to lose her balance and fall into the dusty dirty street. "I've done nothing wrong!" she cried out.

The comments and taunts suddenly stopped. All the town's folk fell silent as Brigid's father pushed his way through the crowd and stood protectively above the defenseless child on the ground.

His stern look caused the villagers to move away whispering among themselves.

Briana's mother spoke loudly and directly at Brigid's father. "Shame on you, Michael Sean O'Grady!"

"You were not to let her in the village!" declared the street sweeper.

Michael O'Grady did not respond. He stooped down, gently lifted his daughter from the dirty roadway and carried her away.

Brianna sadly asked her mother, "Where's she going?"

"Who? That awful girl? Pretend she was never here," her mother demanded.

With those hateful words stinging in their ears, Brigid's father carried her all the way to the safe confines of their little cottage.

21

Home. The sights and smells and sounds: her book on the table, the crackling fire, the aroma of fresh made porridge mingling with the scent of the moist peat walls, the creak of the wooden floor boards – all were very comforting to Brigid as her father placed her down on the wooden chair beside the hearth.

Brigid's mother was quickly upon her with hugs and kisses. Then she examined her daughter to make sure there were no physical injuries. "They've not hurt you, my joy, my blessing, mother's angel, have they?"

Her father handed her mother a bucket of water and a cloth.

Gently washing the dirt from Brigid's hands and face her mother assured her, "You're home now, you're safe."

"They stared at me and they made fun of me." Brigid explained. "That man said I have a hoof not a foot! A hoof like a sheep!" And she began to cry again.

"Brigid listen to me," her father scolded. "Time and time again you were told not to leave this house. One time is one too many."

"It's for your own good," her mother gently added. "Don't you see that now?"

"But they do not know me," Brigid pleaded.

"They were frightened by your foot when you were a babe in my arms. For them nothing has changed," her mother explained.

"Now you know the cruel truth of the world!" her father shouted.

This stunned Brigid. She'd never seen either parent raise their voice in such a manner.

Taking short breaths between sobs, she haltingly pleaded, "Father … I am … so … so sorry!"

"'Tis not with you I am upset," he quickly responded. "My anger is with their ignorance!" After a big sigh, his tone quickly changed. His voice became calm and gentle. "You know your mother and I love you very much," her father continued as he knelt by Brigid's side. "Those people don't know you and what a good person you are."

"If they took the time…" Brigid began, but stopped. She looked at her father looking at her. There was

23

great concern and love in his hazel eyes and she immediately knew he understood what she wanted to say without her saying it.

"Their difficulty is that they don't know what is real from what they imagine. When things are different or strange, well, things unknown, when not ignored, inspire most folk's imaginations to run away with them. Instead of imagining good, they will oft time envision the worse."

"Things different cause fear," her mother added.

"But it's just imagination," Brigid.

"Imagination can make people do the wrong thing," her father gently added.

"That is why we protect you and keep you here," her mother added.

"What is most real is that they could have hurt you. We cannot have it," Sean O'Grady told his daughter. "They are ignorant to believe you are bad, but we cannot change them. So now more than ever you must stay home."

Rinsing the cloth in the pail of water, her mother continued. "You have a life here, Brigid, a life inside these four walls and with your little garden. You'll be sweeping the floor, doing your chores like any other day, and later we'll read a tale from your book."

"That is no longer a good idea," her father explained as he snatched up the book from the table. He paused and drew a deep breath. His resentment of the town's folk and their ignorance overwhelmed his normally gentle nature. His anger caused him to speak more harshly than he would have preferred. Nonetheless, he found himself insisting, "It's this book she's learned to read from. This book has filled her mind with questions. It has given her false hopes and caused restlessness."

Surprised by his forcefulness, Brigid and her mother could not respond.

Shaking the book, her father continued, "These are tales told by liars and lunatics. There is no magic in this world, no fairy fishes and no horses flying over pretty rainbows!"

He threw the book to the floor.

"No-o-o-o!" Brigid shouted as she retrieved the book and hugged it tightly.

25

"It's for the best, child," her father sternly explained. "You will not leave here again to be hurt again. Nor will you ever read another book of wild tales. I must go. I have work in the fields. Mind me now, Brigid. You will stay in this house!"

He left to return to his work, slamming the door behind him.

Brigid stared at the heavy oak door. The silence in the room was only cut by sounds of the fire in the hearth. Brigid could hardly breathe. She had never seen her father in such a state. He had never raised his voice like that.

She continued to stare at the door. Her mother was saying something but she wasn't listening. Brigid was only listening to the thoughts racing through her mind - thoughts of her father's anger mingled with her memories of the villagers' taunts and insults. Brigid's fear slowly changed to anger. It grew inside her until finally she looked away from the oak door and stood up.

"This is no longer home to me. 'Tis a prison!" Brigid called out after her father. "This foot is the cause of it all! If I was like everyone else, I'd be free to walk about and go to school and have friends!"

"Brigid, please. It's not to be," her mother gently informed her and handed Brigid a broom. "Chores, now."

"This foot!" Brigid cried as she threw the broom to the ground. "This foot! This foot! I hate this foot!"

Her mother tried to calm her. "You're our one child. For us every part of you is precious," said she.

Brigid sat and continued holding the book ever so tight.

Her mother shook her head and held out her hand for Brigid to give her the book, but the child refused. She held tightly to the book.

"You'll not be taking my book from me! This is precious to me. It tells me there is hope and magic somewhere in the world. There is! There is!"

She opened the book and showed her Mother. "Here's the gentle caring Sea Mither, who might appear to those who ask. The Sea Mither answers wishes. 'Tis a true story surely!"

"No, darlin', those creatures fly no further than the pages of that book, like dreams in the wake-up world."

Handing her the broom, she continued, "There's the chores to do. The book cannot be here when your father returns. You will see to it."

Her mother picked up the little bucket and left the cottage.

Alone now, Brigid ignored the broom. She opened the book and read out loud.

"The Sea Mither appears over the Cliffs of Moher, a barren place high above the ocean where but few dare travel."

Brigid looked up from the book. "The Cliffs of Moher," she told the empty room, "The Cliffs are not so far from here, only past Googyulla and Doolin. That is where I must go!"

As she stared at the glowing embers in the fireplace, Brigid could hear inside her head a Gaelic incantation that she had seen in the book.: *Ta' draichot anseo. Ta' aochas anseo.*

"Magic is here. Hope is here," Brigid recited out loud. "Ta' draichot anseo. Ta' aochas anseo. Magic is here. Hope is here. Magic is there! My only hope is there!"

She stood up and walked to the door. She touched her mother's apron hanging there on a peg. "Fare thee well mother." She touched her father's old hat. "Goodbye for now father."

Brigid opened the door then turned and looked around the room quickly.

"Farewell house o' my birth and my childhood 'til I return the way I ought to be."

CHAPTER TWO
The Cliffs Of Moher

Brigid walked for maybe an hour and then she heard a horse and cart coming from behind.

Should I hide? She wondered and began to step to the side of the road. But she was too slow in making up her mind and soon the wagon pulled to a stop close to her.

Squinting down at Brigid the old driver asked, "Would you care for a ride?" the old driver asked.

It was obvious that the old man had very poor eyesight and Brigid thought that her foot might not be of any consequence to him.

"Might you be going in the direction of Doolin, sir?"

"'Tis me home, Doolin is."

"My hope is to see the Cliffs of Moher before the sun goes down," she explained.

"That will be no problem, lassie, hop into the back of the hay wagon and rest your feet."

Brigid hopped into the wagon and off they went.

The empty hay wagon moved along at a steady clip and, except for the bouncing around due to the uneven roadway, the journey was pleasant. As they traveled along, the old man shared his lunch of fresh baked bread and dried mutton from a pail on the seat beside him. He even let Brigid have one of his apples.

Not long after they finished their eating, the old man stopped his wagon at a fork in the road.

"Here you go, lassie. 'Tis where we part company. That roadway there? You stay on that road. Walk a good pace and you'll get to the cliffs before the sun sets."

"Bless you sir, and thank you!"

"'Tis a strange place for someone so young to be traveling by herself."

"I won't be alone. I'm to meet someone there who will take care of me."

"I see. Very well then. If you have any problems, should you not find your friend, return to Doolin and find Old David O'Brian. The wife and me would gladly give you shelter."

"That is very kind, sir. Thank you."

With the snap of the reins and shout of "Get on now!" the old man headed off.

Brigid was so excited, she walked up the roadway as quickly as her foot would allow. The afternoon sun was bright and the breeze brought the scent of the sea which was most invigorating. *I must be close!*

As she walked, she marked a cadence reciting the incantation from her book. "Magic is here. Hope is here," Brigid recited out loud as she walked. "Ta' draichot anseo. Ta' aochas anseo. Magic is here. Hope is here! …. Five, six, seven, eight! Magic is there, magic is there, magic is there, I know it!" She repeated it over and over and over until she grew tired of the words. She continued walking along but instead of singing or chanting, she listened to the sounds of the land around her. *So many birds!* She thought. *So many different bird songs!* Several times she heard a rustle in the underbrush then saw a deer or a raccoon bounding across the road. At one point a rabbit darted out of the wood and scampered up the road ahead with a red fox chasing close behind.

"Run, bunny! Run!" Brigid cried out.

The rabbit left the road and disappeared into the underbrush. The fox followed. There was a rustling of the leaves, then silence. Shortly thereafter the fox darted out of the wood and across the road. *Oh good,* Brigid thought. *The bunny must have safely found its warren.*

"Good for you, bunny!" Brigid shouted.

She continued listening to the sounds of the land around her for a while then she recalled another incantation from her book that she had memorized.

She called out the words in a cadence to mark time with her walking pace.

"There is enchantment in the depths of the ocean! There is power in the tides and in the waves. There are wonders in the blues and greens of the waters. There is magic in the briny smell and taste of the seas. There is magic, 'tis magic, that is everywhere."

A breeze blew bringing with it the salty scent of the sea.

It wasn't much later that Brigid could see the ocean in the distance. She picked up her walking pace and soon she arrived at a place where the land gave way to a vast open space with an endless blue ocean at its bottom.

"It's as if I was standing at the very edge of the world!" she whispered to the wind.

The view was enough to take her breath away. The shore was a long, long way straight down. She looked out over the vast ocean and could see the sun was getting closer to the far horizon. The view was breathtaking, but she realized she had little time to spare before night set in.

Firmly planning her feet on the ground and standing as tall as she could, Brigid chanted:

"Dear sea spirits, hear me!

There is enchantment in the depths of the ocean!

There is power in your tides and in the waves.

There are wonders in the blues and greens of the waters.

There is magic in the briny smell and taste of the seas.

Please hear my call!"

Brigid stood very still. The ocean did not change. The waves continued to beat on the rocks far below. The sun was turning orange and the few clouds in the sky began to reflect the colors of sunset.

Nothing happened. The Sea Mither did not appear. Fear began to overtake her. Her thoughts were racing.

What if it is just imagination? Only imagination.

Only imagination, echoed inside her brain. And then she remembered her father's words, "Imagination can make people do the wrong thing,"

"Have I done the wrong thing?" Brigid cried out loud to the sea. Her pulse was pounding in her ears as she recalled her father saying that sometimes imagination makes you think only bad things.

"Unknowns make people think the worst, unknowns cause fear." I think he said that. But does it always have to be? Does that have to be me? I won't do that. Imagination must lead to good things. It must! If you truly believe something to be right and good and not just imagined ... when I believe in good my heart feels lighter. How could something that feels so right be wrong?

Magic is here. Hope is here she remembered. *That I believe.*

35

She heard a seagull's squawk and watched as two gulls went swooping by her and diving down, down, down to the sea.

Suddenly, she heard a bird call from way far away. It was a bird call she did not recognize.

She looked to the west where a sooty tern seemed to fly directly out of the sun. It gracefully swooped down and circled Brigid. Its call was unlike any birdcall Brigid had ever heard. It flew around her three times and then, gently flapping its wings like a hummingbird, the tern hovered in front of Brigid. It had part of a sea shell in its slender black beak.

That bird. It's so beautiful. Why is it staring at me?

"Hello, bird," she found herself saying as if it were perfectly natural to have a conversation with a sooty tern.

The tern's black feathers slowly turned beautiful shades of blues and greens. Its white feathers slowly turned to yellow, orange and red, and all the feathers were glowing.

Oh my.

The tern flew straight up and then swooped back

down. Just as it was about to reach Brigid, it opened its beak and let out a cry that sounded like a riff on a penny whistle. This caused the shell to drop from its mouth, hit Brigid square on the head and bounce to the ground at her feet.

"Hey!" Brigid shouted as the sooty tern flew off into the sun.

That bird. That bird meant for me to have this shell.

She looked down. It was part of a large sea scallop shell. Its grooves fanned out from its one flat side and there were lines of dull tan, brown, white and gray across the grooves.

Not very colorful, she thought as she picked it up. But turning it over in her hands she saw that the underside had a polished sheen and featured a random array of shiny colors.

This is a part of the sea. Why has that bird given me a part of the sea? Maybe ...

With both hands, Brigid held the shell high above her head and chanted:

37

"Dear sea spirits, hear me!

There is enchantment in the depths of your ocean!

There is power in your tides and in your waves.

There are wonders in the blues and greens of your waters.

There is magic in the briny smell and taste of your seas.

Please hear my call!"

With all of her strength, she then threw the shell out over the ocean and watched as it fell and then shattered on the rocks below.

She waited.

A very large gray cloud of mist began to swirl below the cliffs. The wind shifted. It began to blow from the sea. Brigid took a deep breath of the cool moist air, and letting it out she continued her plea, calling as loudly as she could, "Sea Mither! Hear me! I was born with this difference unlike everyone else. I hate this body of mine which is made ugly and weak. I hate this head of mine which is made confused. I hate this heart of mine which

38

feels only anger and despair. Help me, Sea Mither! Bring me your hope, Sea Mither! Bring me your magic!

The swirling cloud of mist grew larger and larger. Its gray color slowly turned to lavender with streaks of pink and green and yellow. Sea spirits and sprites seemed to fly and dance in and around the cloud. Brigid's jaw dropped, her eyes grew wide and she almost forgot to breathe as she watched the Sea Mither rise gracefully from the sea.

Sea spirits and sprites seemed to be darting every which way, and the light of the setting sun cast a glow on it all, especially the Sea Mither's beautiful long auburn hair.

Brigid was almost at a loss for words. "Oh my. Oh my," Brigid uttered at the sight.

The beautiful Sea Mither gazed upon Brigid with her soft green eyes and smiled the most gentle of loving smiles. "Child, I hear your cry. Tell me your wish."

"I want this one foot of mine to be like the other, and like everyone else's. You'll change how people look upon me and they'll like me. They will. Change this ugly foot of mine, please!"

"I can see into your heart, dear girl, and this is truly your desire."

"Oh, it is! It is!"

"Then three be the number of tests you must endure and then you will reach the person for wishes asked and wisely answered."

"You're not the person? Why not?"

"Dear Brigid, there is more to a wish than the wishing. Not only must you ask, you must show yourself worthy."

"How? Outside my home the others are mean to me because I am different. I don't want to be different!"

"I understand your plea, but do you understand you must prove yourself worthy?"

"How can I do that?"

"It is a hard way, a testing way. Do you dare?"

Brigid stared at the wonders before her – the sea sprites and the beautiful woman with long auburn hair, green eyes and a silky robe of blues and greens floating on the wind. Brigid watched as all of the sea spirits and sprites suddenly stopped to hover almost motionless as they waited for Brigid's reply. She swallowed. She took a deep breath, looked directly at the Sea Mither and said, "I will do what needs the doing!"

In the blink of an eye, the sea sprites placed a wooden staff of highly polished oak at Brigid's feet. It was about half a meter long and about as thick as three of Brigid's fingers.

"Ah then, you'll take this Bard's Rod. It will be your compass."

Brigid took up the rod and marveled at the intricate designs carved into it along with the Gaelic words: "Ta' draichot anseo. Ta' aochas anseo."

"I know this! Magic is here. Hope is here!" Brigid sang out.

"I can only help you help yourself," said the Sea Mither as she leaned forward and kissed Brigid on the forehead. "It will point the way. The rest is up to you."

"Thank you!"

"Breathe deep now," the Sea Mither instructed. "You will tap the rod to the earth three times as you deliver an incantation."

"I am ready!"

"Look to where the sea meets the sky, dear Brigid Shawn O'Grady. Listen to the waves upon the rocks far below. Hold the Bard's Rod tightly, tap and recite:

"Tap once, twice, thrice.

Bard's Rod, point the way to the well at world's edge.

Point the way to what I need.

Point the way."

Brigid recited along with the Sea Mither. Suddenly, as if controlled by an invisible hand, the Bard's Rod pulled on her arm and made her twirl around and then stop abruptly. Like the needle of a compass, it pointed straight out over the sea.

"Follow it without a swerve or a curve," the Sea Mither crooned.

"But ... but," Brigid protested and dropped the rod to the ground. "It points out over the cliff into thin air!"

"There's magic here and hope," the Sea Mither

assured her. "You must follow it through three tests. Follow it and prove yourself worthy."

Brigid's knees began to tremble and her stomach tightened in a knot. "I cannot. My bones will be broken on the rocks below, and I will be drowned."

The Sea Mither ignored Brigid's fears and simply crooned, "Follow it to the well at world's edge."

"There's magic here and hope," the sea sprites chanted.

Brigid hesitantly picked up the Rod and it instantly pointed out over the cliff.

"There's magic here," the Sea Mither sang.

"The magic is real!" Brigid cried out as if to assure herself.

"And hope is here," chanted the sprites.

Brigid called out, "Hope is all I have!" She gripped the rod tightly and stepped to the very edge of the cliff. She took a deep breath of the cool sea air, spread her arms wide and leaned so far forward she began to fall.

Brigid fell down and down, and as she fell the Sea Mither hovered directly in front of her. Brigid looked down and saw the rocks and the crashing sea below and was very frightened. She looked up to plead to the Sea Mither but she saw the Sea Mither smiling a most loving smile and offering her hands. Brigid reached out. They clasped hands and Brigid suddenly felt very safe. Together they fell until they almost touched the water and then the Sea Mither pulled Brigid close and they flew along the top of the ocean.

She did not look back, so Brigid was not aware of the Cliffs of Moher receding further and further away until they were flying out over the open ocean. *The Bard's Rod! Where did it go? She wondered. And then reaching down she found it securely tucked into her belt.*

Putting that worry aside, she looked around and marveled at the sight of flying fish, sea sprites and other sea creatures encircling her and the Sea Mither. She reached down and let her hand touch the top of waves.

Then with a big kerplunk! the Sea Mither, Brigid, the sea sprites and numerous sea creatures all dove into the sea!

Brigid held her breath and marveled at the sights

around her. *Is that a shark or a mermaid? A dolphin or a sea-fairy? Never have I seen such colorful sea forms and creatures!*

Hundreds of them swarmed around and around her and then disappeared.

I am in the water, but oh, 'tis cold but dry like make-believe. Am I swimming? ...floating?...sinking? ...can I be dreaming it all? If I am not in water, where am I?

She took a deep breath. She looked left and she looked right. The Sea Mither had vanished, leaving Brigid alone and tumbling over and over in such a fashion that she was unsure if she was moving side to side or up or down. *Am I slipping or sliding, floating or flying? Whatever it is, I am not getting dizzy. I am not getting wet. Up or down or side-to-side, it seems all the same. North is south or left is right or am I wrong? Is it a minute that has gone by? ...an hour? ...perhaps a day? It seems almost forever or is it no more than the blink of an eye?*

Brigid continued floating until the underwater world dissolved into a bright shiny day and she gently landed on a vast sandy beach on the edge of an ocean.

The Sea Mither returned and hovered above the gently rolling waves.

"Three be the number of tests. Pass the three tests and then you will reach the well at the world's edge and the sage. The sage is the person for wishes asked and wisely answered. Are you ready?"

"I will do what needs doing." said Brigid with all the certainty she could muster.

"And so, it begins!" the Sea Mither sang out.

She then dove into the water and disappeared.

Brigid looked around and about. He boots, her clothes and her hair were all dry. And she was all alone. Or at least she thought she was all alone.

CHAPTER THREE
A Kelpie

Brigid looked up and down what seemed to be a long and empty beach.

... empty except for that large rock with a lot of sand all over it, she thought.

As she walked closer to the rock, she realized that she was not as much frightened of her new surroundings as she was confused.

Where in the world ... or where out of the world, am I? Is this a world of wondrous adventures and mysteries or a very lonely and very empty place?

"And that's really a heavy rope all over that big rock," she observed out loud.

With each step, her boots sank a little into the sand causing her to wonder about this very different place.

Even the dirt is different.

The look of it, even the feel of it, was unlike anything she had walked on back home in County Clare.

"It's not as firm and it makes a crunching sound,"

she told the air. "Nothing seems to be growing in this kind of soil. What is it?"

She reached down and gathered a handful of sand.

Tiny stones. White, brown, pink, yellow ... so many shades of yellow. I imagine these were rocks once. Rocks tumbling in the sea for years and years and years.

She took a seat on the "rock" only to have it instantly wriggle its way out from under her.

"Get off of me!"

"Oh! So sorry," Brigid exclaimed as she landed on the soft yellow sand.

"Sorry? For plunking your lumpy little self upon me? Do I look like a chair to you?"

"No, but ... you're not a rock!" *It's some creature all tied up.*

"A slip, a zip!" the creature sputtered as it tumbled over and over. "A zig, a zag, umph! ... and I will be ... free!" The creature strained against the ropes then stopped. "Oh, bother!"

The creature then started rocking back and forth. "Any time now! One, two three!" And it began to tumble over and over.

Brigid could see that under that snarl of hemp rope were four legs with hooves. She could see that it had short fur, but its many colors created the appearance of sparkling fish scales.

Under all that rope something is certainly shimmering like when fish scales catch the rays of the sun.

There was also a flowing golden mane and large head that was horse-like.

Could someone have tied a large fish to a horse?

Then she realized ... "You're a kelpie!" Brigid shouted.

"A very angry ... umph ... and frustrated kelpie if you please!" the creature growled back at her.

Brigid quickly snatched one end of the rope and pulled very hard. This action freed up the kelpie's front legs, but his hind legs, head and neck remained tight against his body by the coils of hemp rope.

"Do let me help ..." Brigid started to say and reached out and petted the kelpie between its ears and tussled his blonde forelock. "You're going to be okay ..."

The kelpie started to giggle. The more Brigid played with the kelpie's forelock, the harder the animal laughed.

"Stop!" he gasped between laughs. "Stop tickling me!!"

Brigid quickly removed her hand. "A kelpie who is ticklish?"

"Isn't everyone?"

"I just want to help," she started to explain and dropped both hands to her sides.

"Tickling doesn't help!" he exclaimed.

"That's true. But perhaps if I…"

"Hah! You? Do you actually think I need your help? I am strong! I am swift! I am smart!"

"Pardon me, kelpie sir, but if you are so strong and swift and smart, how did you get all tied up and …"

"I was tricked!" He explained as he continued wrestling with his bonds. "Ten fierce, no twenty fierce demons equipped with weapons galore! Their knives and axes were sharp and magical! Thirty fierce and sneaky demons it was who attacked me all-of-a-sudden! They

came at me from behind ... and in the dark! And ... and ... a
spell was put upon me!"

"It must have been a very powerful spell to bind a
magical creature such as yourself."

"The most powerful of spells, yes! I could not
move a muscle! I could not speak or even twitch an ear! It
allowed those demons to paralyze me so completely!"

"How long have you been ..."

"Days! Nights! Weeks and weeks! But I will be
free of this impediment now! NOW!" And the kelpie
strained so hard against the ropes that his head turned
bright pink.

"That didn't work," observed Brigid. "If you'll be
still, I will try to help you."

The kelpie continued to struggle with the ropes,
tumbling over and over and becoming one big ball of rope
and kelpie sweat and sand.

"You dare help me?" he grumbled, "You mushy-
hearted mealy-minded fluttery buttery <u>human</u>? Hah! A
slip, a dip, a zig and a zag and ... I'll ... be ... Ah! I will not
be mortified by a simple, mindless coil of hemp!"

He stopped twisting turning and tugging and stared at Brigid.

"You had better go on your way, lass. I must warn you that when I snap this trap - and I will … in less than a minute! …and all of my hoofs will be free, I will be very nasty! I cannot help myself because I am almighty mean, I am! I… I …"

But the kelpie suddenly fainted from exhaustion.

Brigid stepped back, looked down at the kelpie lying so still in the yellow sand and announced, "I'll be gone, I shall."

She turned away, but did not take a step.

She turned back around, and bending over him, reconsidered. *Oh, the poor dear.*

She started to reach out to the kelpie, but quickly withdrew her hand and considered the situation.

He is a kelpie, she reminded herself. *You know what they say about kelpies. In my book, there is a story about a kelpie who is a hateful trickster and nasty with his every word. He'll trick me and there's the chance that he will hurt me.*

She stepped back from the kelpie and seriously considered going on her way. She took the Bard's Rod from her belt and was about to tap three times when she thought again.

Oh, but he's tied up and so tired. When the tide comes in he will be covered in water and unable to swim and he could drown. If I leave him like this, he will surely die.

A debate continued in her mind. *Should I help him or let him be? I could easily untie those ropes.*

Leave him!

Should I?

He is defenseless. Help him!

What if I untied those ropes and he tricked me into riding into the sea so I will drown? That's the legend about kelpies. But are all kelpies evil? I am unsure. This might be a situation where an unknown is actually evil. Therefore, I best leave him.

She took a step away then stopped.

But he is defenseless! What if this is a situation where an unknown is good?

53

She weighed the good against the bad. The bad possibilities came to mind more easily than the good.

Father was correct. It is so much easier to imagine bad about the unknown. It takes determination to imagine the good. This is very interesting.

Good. Bad. Good. Bad. Thoughts tumbled one after another. Back and forth her thoughts went and finally it came down to two possible paths for Brigid to take.

Shall I believe what's in my head? All kelpies are nasty and can harm you and forget him? Or shall I believe what's in my heart?

"If I leave him, he will surely die!" she yelled out to the sea.

Of course, the sea was not helpful. The waves rolled in. The waves tumbled out. Their sounds, along with the chirping of a tern or two, were all the sounds heard until Brigid announced to the sea, "I can't! No, I cannot bring myself to leave him to die!"

So Brigid carefully approached the rope ensnarled kelpie and cautiously untied the rope that bound him. Then she stepped back.

Should I run away now?

Her curiosity kept her at that spot. She watched as the kelpie groaned and began to stir. He slowly realized his limbs were free.

"Ah hah!" he cried out. He leapt up and flipped head over tail shouting, "Free!" He then flipped again. "Oh! Ah! Free!" he shouted.

He was jumping and laughing and celebrating his victory when he realized that Brigid was staring at him.

He stopped his gleeful dance and addressed her sternly. "I was one minute away from freeing myself. Isn't that what it looked like to you?"

"Oh. Uh. Surely." *He certainly is unusually proud of himself.*

"It was a spell, I tell you! It was an unbreakable, blinding deafening dumbing paralyzing spell that I broke! Another legendary feat for the kelpie! Zip zap hip hop swing swoop!" he sang out as he danced about and punched the air with his front hoofs. "Bring on the demons, fiends, monsters!" he called out.

Then he stopped his happy dance.

"My strength is impressive, is it not?" he asked Brigid directly. "Strength! I am very powerful. I could hit you and kick you and bite you until it hurts. I could I could I could!"

"I'll be on my way then," Brigid meekly replied.

"Stop," the kelpie shouted. "Do you know where you are? Don't answer that. Why am I talking to you? You are totally insignificant. Humans are so strange with their next-to-nothing nose and ears, and with hands and feet that don't match. Ugh! Not enough hair to cover yourself. Soft, slow, and, in your case, KIND! No use denying it!" He shook his head in utter disgust. "And then," he added, pointing to her foot, "you've got that odd foot there."

Brigid shouted defensively, "It's my ugly, misshapen foot!" And she turned and started walking away.

"Stop!" the kelpie shouted. "I meant the tiny one. The other foot, the big one, it looks as nice as one of mine!"

Brigid stopped and turned to face the kelpie.

"It's the only thing on you that's pretty," he

snorted. "But, except for the pretty foot, you are, well, <u>human</u>."

Again, he pranced around her, showing off and chanting, "Beautiful legs! ... beautiful eyes! ... beautiful me! Zip zap hip hop swing swoop!" He stopped and stared at her. "You will never make it on your own. Do you know where you're going?"

"Wherever this points me," she explained, holding out the Bard's Rod.

"Ah, the Bard's Rod. That it is. I am sure it takes some reciting, does it not?"

Brigid look at him. She wasn't sure if he was making fun of her or not, but she proceeded to recite and tap the rod to the earth.

"Tap once, twice, thrice.

Bard's Rod, point the way to the well at world's edge.

Point the way to what I need.

Point the way."

Brigid twirled around until the rod stopped her

abruptly. "That's the way."

"I see," observed the kelpie, "that it points in the general direction of the well at the world's edge. Off to see the old woman, the Sage, are you?"

"That is precisely where I am going to go. Good day." Once again, Brigid turned and started walking away.

"Don't beg," the kelpie called out to her. "I will help you."

"You?! No!" Brigid scolded. "Why would I want the help of a nasty, rubbish-mouth kelpie?"

"Why? Because you are a hopeless human! Because with all the hardships you're bound to face, you might need my brains, my strength and my cunning. Wanna ride, wanna ride, wanna ride?" he chanted, hopping up and down and then kneeling to make it easy for Brigid to hop on his back.

Brigid hesitated.

"Hop on and give your beautiful foot a rest!"

"I've read," she told him, "that a kelpie might trick a human by offering them a ride, but when they are riding the kelpie dives down to the deepest part of the ocean so that the rider drowns!"

"You have? Oh. That must be my cousin. I don't do that."

Brigid looked at him for a moment then asked, "How do I know that for certain?"

"Think about where your magic stick is pointing." And with that he stood up on his hind legs so he could gesture with his front hooves. "Is it pointing to the sea? No. It is pointing inland, away from the sea," he announced dramatically. "And, most important, think about this ... who am I? ... I am a simple kelpie. What right would I have to defy a Bard's Rod? None. I will not defy a Bard's Rod. You understand?"

"Well, I think I do," Brigid explained.

Once again, the kelpie knelt down and gestured for Brigid to hop onto his back. "Up you go!"

She did not move.

He's made a very good point. But what if it's just part of his trickery?

"Hello!" the kelpie shouted. "I'm thinking that you don't trust the Bard's Rod as much as I do."

"Oh, I do!"

"You think I would defy it? Hah! There will not be much drowning," he explained most sincerely. "I promise, no sea-dunking, no river-plunking. Besides, it would be very difficult to drown you in a field of heather, wouldn't you think? Ha!"

Brigid climbed up on his back.

"Good! Now hold tight."

Brigid grabbed a handful of the kelpie's golden mane.

"And off we go!" he shouted as he galloped off in the direction the Bard's Rod had pointed. "And so 'tis to be written," he sang out, "the brave kelpie, swift and strong, carried the helpless young lass on her quest beyond the sandy shore and into the countryside."

The sounds of the sea grew distant as they journeyed inland over the gently rolling hills of the greenest pastureland Brigid had ever seem. They passed wild goats grazing and frolicsome rabbits.

Is that goat blue? Did that rabbit snarl at me and wink? It was a wonder.

On and on they went. There was open land as far as she could see.

No houses or barns ... or fences, she thought. *There are no boys nor another girl, no grownups in sight.*

Brigid closed her eyes and enjoyed the warm wind upon her face. *Is this what it feels like to fly?*

She tensed her legs, tightening her knee's grip on the kelpie's body. She took a deep breath and, without opening her eyes, she let go of his mane and spread her arms out to her sides. She imagined she had wings.

The sun, the breeze, this is magical! Refreshing is the word! Refreshing as a cool cup of well water on a hot day ... and very exciting! Scary, too!

"Woohoo!" Brigid howled.

"Do you like this?" the kelpie asked.

"Yes! Oh so very much, yes!" she shouted.

"You're not scared?"

"It's exciting-scary," she responded with some certainty. "like the first time I climbed so high up in the tall oak tree near my home ... so high up that the branches were barely strong enough to hold me! Yes! Exciting-scary!"

"Gravity wanted you on the ground. Who won? You? Gravity?"

"Me!" she exclaimed with a laugh.

With her eyes still closed and arms extended, Brigid concentrated on the steady rhythm of the kelpie's body as he galloped along. Little by little she began to match that tempo with simple movements. She leaned slightly forward, then up and then back matching the movement and tempo of the Kelpie's gallop. Forward, up and back and forward and up and back and forward and up and back … over and over again and again.

Then she shouted, "Ta' draichot anseo. Ta' aochas anseo! Magic is here! Hope is here!"

Her heart soared.

She rode along silently for a short while, wanting this new sense of freedom to last forever. But suddenly a new sound broke her reverie. The sound of the ocean.

Have we gone in a circle?

Her eyes snapped open in panic. She grabbed a handful of the kelpie's golden mane and looked around.

It was fantastic! As they rode along, the landscape changed in an instant from one climate to another as if the earth was playing a game of "let's pretend."

Is that the roar of the cold ocean I hear?

Turning to the right, she saw they were surrounded by sand and there were tall breaking waves in the distance. She blinked.

Is that the hot wind of the desert I feel on my face?

Suddenly they were galloping up a gigantic sand dune and she could see the lush palm trees of a desert oasis not too far ahead. She blinked.

Now it is cool ... and where's the sun?

The desert had disappeared and they were now trotting on a dirt road winding through a forest of the tallest trees Brigid had ever seen.

Then, in another blink of an eye, it all became pasture lands again. They passed field after field of lush farmland. There were fields of grain and pasturelands with grazing sheep. But the sheep were unlike sheep she'd ever seen before. Some sheep were red, some were blue and some were yellow.

"Back home, the sheep are white," said Brigid.

"All the time?" the Kelpie asked.

"Occasionally, a black one …"

"How are you able to make a blue coat or a red scarf?" he asked her in disbelief.

"Oh, I see. How easier it must be … and so different."

"You miss your home already," the kelpie declared. "You want to go back, I knew it."

"Of course, I miss my home. But no. Here is where I must be for now. It is all so curious."

Soon the sun was setting. The kelpie was getting tired so he slowed to a walk then paused to rest on the side of the road in front of a farmhouse.

The kelpie kneeled, Brigid jumped off and they both settled down on the grass by the road.

"Liam! Come quick! It's a kelpie!" Brigid heard a woman cry.

"Uh oh," Brigid sighed.

"There's a kelpie in the front yard! Get your crossbow!"

Brigid jumped up from the lawn, hopped up on the Kelpie's back and started rubbing his forelock. It being his ticklish spot, the Kelpie started laughing. She kept rubbing and he laughed even louder.

"Stop! Stop!" the Kelpie cried and then laughed some more.

The farmer appeared in the farmhouse doorway next to his wife. The two of them stared for a moment. Brigid kept tickling and the Kelpie kept laughing.

"Can't be a true evil kelpie, Katherine," the famer told his wife. "The evil ones don't know how to laugh." And he put down his cross bow.

"Hello!" called Brigid as she hopped off the Kelpie's back. "He's very friendly as you can see."

The Kelpie rolled over on the grass trying desperately to catch his breath.

"That … was not … called … for!" he managed to screech between breaths.

"Yes, it was," Brigid hissed back at him. She then turned to the farmer and his wife. "We've been traveling a long way. Might we drink from your well?"

"Better still, you can join us for the evening meal, my dear. We'd be happy to share our supper."

The young farmer and his kindly wife insisted the Kelpie join them as well. He was most gracious about that and even entertained them with a story of how he came to be rescued by Brigid. Acting out all the parts; he told how the three evil goblins, two nasty gremlins along with five, no six! … six gnomes tricked him, took his gold and left him tied up on a beach! He was moaning and rolling around on the floor pretending he was all tied up.

"Then I found him and helped him escape all those ropes!" Brigid chimed in.

"That she did even though I was particularly nasty towards her," the Kelpie added. "And that's the end of my tale," the Kelpie added as he got up from the floor and took a deep bow.

The farmer, his wife and Brigid applauded. The Kelpie took another bow and was rewarded with three carrots which he immediately devoured.

By the time they finished a hearty meal, exchanged a few funny stories and laughed together, the sun was close to setting so the farmer's wife told them, "You're welcome, travelers, to stay on our farm for the night."

"'Tis only hay for a pillow in the barn of our humble farm," her husband added.

"That will be fine, sir," Brigid responded.

The farmer led them to the barn where he spread an old blanket over some straw and the farmer's wife brought them a quilt for cover.

"It will surely be nice to be able to sleep with a roof over our heads," Brigid explained. "Thank you so much!"

Wishing them all a good night's sleep, the farmer and his wife closed the big barn door and returned to their home.

Everyone settled down and slept soundly through the night.

CHAPTER FOUR
A Giant Test

Brigid awoke very early the next morning.

After a good stretch like a cat would do when waking up, Brigid settled on her back in the straw and stared up at the puffy clouds in the bright blue sky above. The morning sun was painting them with streaks of pink and red and orange and yellow. She could hear the cows mooing and the sheep bleating in the pasture not too far away, and the chickens clucking in the dooryard beyond the barn door.

Hmm, she thought, looking to her right, *didn't they close that barn door last night?* Then looking up, she remarked out loud, "Oh, what lovely clouds," Brigid sighed.

"Clouds?" asked the kelpie as he began to wake. "What clouds?"

"Those clouds." Brigid pointed straight up. "Looks to be the start of a lovely day."

The kelpie was enjoying the sight when he suddenly realized. "Why is the roof gone?"

"Roof?" Brigid asked. Then she sat straight up and yelled, "Roof! Kelpie, what happened to the roof?"

"I slept so deeply," he explained, "that I heard nothing through the night."

"Right. No big wind in the night, but I remember I did hear a loud sneeze this morning. I thought I was dreaming."

"Just a sneeze?" the kelpie asked her. "Like a great big sneeze?"

"Yes, a giant sneeze," she answered him.

"Giant!" They both yelled and jumped to their feet.

The farmer and his wife came running from the house and stopped where the big barn door once hung.

"Giant!" the farmer managed to shout while panting for breath.

"Help us!" his wife exclaimed.

"Who me? I can't do anything." Brigid responded.

"You're the one with the wand!" the farmer shouted.

"This?" Brigid asked, holding up the Bard's Rod.

"Looks like a magic wand to me," he continued. "Use it to get rid of the giant, please! Make him smaller before he hurts anyone."

"This Bard's Rod isn't a magic wand. It just points the way."

"You have to help us! Give it a try," he pleaded. "The giant will eat all of our cows and sheep!"

"And our chickens!" the farmer's wife added.

Brigid examined the Bard's Rod wondering aloud, "I haven't had it that long, so I don't know all it can do." She held up the Bard's Rod. "I think it is just a compass of sorts.

"Ouch!" Brigid cried out. The Bard's Rod so quickly moved to point at the farmer's stomach that it pulled on Brigid's arm.

"It's pointing to his stomach," the farmer's wife exclaimed. "Don't hurt him!"

"What does that mean?" the farmer asked his wife.

Brigid looked at the rod, looked at the farmer and back at the rod. She then asked the man, "What did you eat this morning?"

"Nothing, yet!" the farmer grumbled.

"Um, people ..." the kelpie tried to interrupt.

"I prepared a whole lot of griddle cakes," his wife boasted.

"... stacks and stacks of griddle cakes!" the farmer added.

"Hello? Giant coming ..." the kelpie reminded them.

Suddenly they heard a big crash that sounded as if it was coming from the next farm down the lane. They ran out of the barn to have a look.

Suddenly they heard a big splash.

"Look!" cried the farmer's wife, "his one foot is past that hill, where McNamara's pond used to be!"

And then there was a splintering crash!

"His other foot is over there where their barn used to be," yelled the farmer.

From a distance they heard the voice of the giant.

"Ha ha ha! Squish! Squash! Fun fun fun!"

"'Tis my chance to be a hero," boasted the kelpie shaking a fist in the giant's direction. "The legend will say kelpie conquers giant!"

Then crash! Part of a chicken coop fell from the sky and crashed to the ground just missing the kelpie.

"Don't hold me back!" the kelpie shouted as he held tightly to Brigid. "Kelpie saves farmer and wife with his dazzling speed and his mighty muscularity!" He hugged Brigid even tighter shouting, "I'll not be stopped! Zip zap hip hop swing swoop!"

"Don't you see? 'Tis a test, surely," Brigid explained to her hoofed companion.

"Ah, well then. I'll not be interfering," replied the kelpie. "'Til you fail. Giant, big and strong and ugly. You, little and weak and ugly."

"But I must do something!" Brigid explained as she untangled herself from the kelpie's grip. "Let go of me!"

"Kelpie!" the farmer's wife shouted. "Use your magic!"

"Me? I can't do magic. I just am magic," he insisted.

"Brigid, lass, your magic wand! Try it!" shouted the farmer.

"The Bard's Rod! Yes. Thank you!" She paused for a very brief moment to consider the Bard's Rod. "Stomach!" shouted Brigid. "Griddle cakes!" she added. "Go, ma'am, please! Go to the house and bring me lots of griddle cakes! Go go go!"

The farmer's wife hurried to the house followed by her husband.

"Bring me the griddle cakes and we will get rid of the giant. Trust me!"

As they watched the farmer and his wife run into their little house, Brigid and the kelpie felt the earth shake.

"Trust me, and leave!" cried the kelpie.

"We might be able to trick the giant," she assured him.

"We might be eaten!" the kelpie protested.

"Not if my plan works! Give me your shoes!"

"What?"

"Please give me two of your shoes," Brigid asked nicely.

"Please give me the magic stick," the kelpie demanded. "Point the way away from here, now!"

"That's not the proper way, Kelpie!" Brigid insisted.

"The right way is far away!" the kelpie corrected her.

"The proper way is to help these people," Brigid scolded him.

"But there's a giant!" he whined.

"Give me your shoes! I know how to get rid of him!"

"No!" the kelpie insisted as he sat down on all four of his hooves.

"You said you would help me! Now help me help these people!" Brigid demanded.

At that moment the farmer and his wife hurriedly returned. She was carrying a pan stacked high with griddle cakes and he carried a dish that held several more. They were the best-looking griddle cakes Brigid had ever seen.

"They look delicious!" cried the kelpie.

"We will let you have one if you give me two of your metal shoes," Brigid declared.

"Well …"

"Giant! Closer!" yelled the farmer.

"Two shoes, two griddle cakes!" said the kelpie.

"That is so selfish!" Brigid scolded.

"But I am so hungry. Two cakes. Please?" whined the kelpie.

"Please cooperate! I know this will work. I know it. Now, please, the three of you," Brigid instructed. "Don't run, don't speak. What I am going to tell the giant is really going to sound silly. DO NOT say anything. Understand? Just nod!"

The farmer and his wife nodded.

Brigid turned to the kelpie. "I still need your shoes!"

"Do I get to have some griddle cakes? Those are really good-looking griddle cakes."

"I promise we will save you some! Just you keep still and ...."

But she stopped talking because she noticed a very large and menacing shadow had overtaken them. The alarmed expressions on the farmer and his wife's faces told Brigid that they had company. Large company.

Brigid turned and found that she was looking at the biggest pair of boots she had ever seen in her life.

"Hello, little people!" said the giant.

"Hello!" shouted Brigid.

"I'm going to step on you," roared the giant. "And you, and you, and you, and kill you and suck upon your tiny bones!"

Brigid took a deep breath, looked up at the giant and exclaimed as bravely as she could, "You do not want to do that."

The giant laughed very loudly, "Ha ha ha!" Smiling down at Brigid he said, "Of course I do! I'm really big and you are very small. It will be so much fun! You will go squish and squirt and be flat and dead. Ha ha ha!"

"If you do that," Brigid calmly explained, "my father will have to squish you dead. He'll soon be home, he will."

The kelpie hissed at Brigid asking, "Your father?!"

"My father," she hissed back, then shouted up to the giant, "Yes, my father the extra strong and extra-large giant."

"Her father is a giant?" the farmer whispered to his wife in astonishment.

"No harm letting him think so," she whispered back nodding toward the giant.

Brigid then boasted, "He's truly a giant among giants, my father is!"

"Bigger than me?" asked the giant with a hearty laugh. "Ha ha ha!"

"Oh, surely. In fact, I myself shall be your small size in about two weeks."

"Two weeks?" asked the giant. "Well now, how old might you be?"

"I am seven-days-old," Brigid proudly exclaimed.

"How can that be?" the giant asked. "You can walk and you can talk."

"We are a very healthy family," Brigid explained. Then, pointing to the farmer and his wife, she added, "My cousins here, they're only twelve-days-old! In another week I'll be high as those trees. And in a month, we will be as tall as that mountain over there."

"But I am hungry. Can I eat just one of your cousins?"

"No."

"The shorter one?"

"No!" shouted Brigid.

I don't believe you," shouted the giant, "so I will stomp on you now and squash you flat just for the fun of it."

Brigid ignored his comment and continued weaving her tale.

"See those sheep over there? My giant father will soon be starting his breakfast by eating five or ten of those sheep.

"I eat sheep, me too," the giant boasted. "Just watch me!" He turned away to examine the sheep. Pondering the flock, he asked. "Which of them is the biggest, fattest of them all? Let me see."

"Not my sheep," whimpered the farmer's wife.

"So sorry, ma'am," Brigid whispered. "But I will get rid of him shortly."

The giant began poking each of the sheep one after the other to decide which he would eat.

Brigid did not want the giant to eat the sheep, so she worked very fast. She ran at the kelpie and pushed him over. "Feet up!" she insisted.

"Ow!" the kelpie exclaimed as he fell on his side. "What are you doing?"

"I need two of your horseshoes."

"Why?"

"Do not argue! Give them to me! Quick! While he is distracted!"

Not too far away the giant continued poking the sheep with his big fat finger.

"Bah. Baah. Baaah!" the sheep protested with each poke.

As the kelpie struggled to remove a shoe from his rear left hoof, Brigid used all of her strength and pulled the horseshoe off of his rear right hoof.

"Ouch! Ooh! My shoe!"

"Shush!" Brigid whispered. "Stop complaining. I need them for the giant."

"Give me back my two griddle cakes!" Kelpie hissed.

"What can a giant do with horseshoes?" asked the farmer's wife.

"I'm in need of metal," whispered Brigid as she snatched the horseshoe the kelpie was holding in his two front hooves.

"Not that one, too!" exclaimed the kelpie. But Brigid ignored him. She turned to the farmer's wife and took the pan of griddle cakes from her hands.

"Why is she taking your griddle cakes?" asked the farmer.

"You'll see," Brigid answered as she set the pan on the ground and tossed two griddle cakes to the kelpie. Brigid then carefully stuffed a horseshoe into the top griddle cake. Next, she took the plate of griddle cakes from the farmer and did the same with the top cake on his pile.

"So many sheep!" the giant uttered. "I cannot decide. But oh, I think I will eat all of them starting with that one!" He picked up the biggest fattest sheep.

"Baaaaaah!" the sheep cried.

He was about to bite it when Brigid called out to him.

"Oh, mister giant! Here! Have something more delicious! Here! My father eats these every morning. Look here!"

"Oh," the giant exclaimed, putting the sheep down. "A horsey with pretty colors!"

Brigid realized he was pointing at the kelpie.

"Why is he pointing at me?" the kelpie hissed. He then tried to hide behind the two griddle cakes he was holding.

"I will eat the horsey with all the pretty colors!" the giant exclaimed as he scooped up the kelpie in his giant hand. "Yum."

"Hey! Let go! Let go!" the kelpie shrieked.

"Put him down!" Brigid yelled.

"Why?" asked the giant. "I want to eat him."

"My father, the giant of giants, only eats animals for dessert. Before he eats a horsey he eats about a hundred of these griddle cakes. These are special griddle cakes made only for the giant of giants."

"Special giant's griddle cakes?" the giant asked. "I like griddle cakes. I want some!"

"Here's two cakes now. Open wide!" the kelpie shouted.

The giant opened his mouth and the kelpie tossed his two griddle cakes so they landed on the giant's big tongue.

"These are delicious! I want more!" exclaimed the giant.

"Those were kelpie griddle cakes. I can't let you have my father's griddle cakes. They are only for the giant of giants," Brigid explained.

"Yes, you can, yes you will, yes, yes, yes!" the giant demanded.

"We have no more of those kelpie griddle cakes," Brigid insisted.

"You better or else I will eat the sheep and the horsey at the same time!"

"NO!" Brigid shouted. "Put the horsey and the sheep down and I will give you all of these special giant's griddle cakes," Brigid explained as she held up the pan holding the stack of golden cakes.

"I like griddle cakes," the giant exclaimed as he dropped the kelpie and the sheep to the ground. He then snatched the top four griddle cakes from the offered stack.

"They are very tough, the way her giant father likes them," the farmer bravely shouted. He then turned to his wife and whispered, "Have you ever seen hands that big before? He's popped four cakes into his mouth like they were no bigger than a gumdrop!"

"Hush, man, hush!" she whispered back.

Suddenly they heard a "crack!" and the giant shouted, "Ouch!" and a large table-sized tooth fell out of the giant's mouth and landed on the ground near Brigid.

"Ochy ouch, ouch, ouch! That griddle cake. It broke my tooth!" the giant roared.

"That's strange," observed Brigid. "That's what

my father, the giant of giants, eats every morning. He eats dozens and dozens."

"That father of yours must be very strong," the Giant said.

"Tough as iron," yelled the kelpie. "Tougher than you!"

"Not possible!" shouted the giant.

"I don't understand how it could have broken your tooth," said Brigid as she took the next four griddle cakes off the stack in the pan and handed one each to the farmer, his wife and the kelpie. She kept one for herself and took a very big bite out of it. "My cousins and I – even the horsey - have no trouble eating these wonderful golden griddle cakes," she explained even though she knew it was impolite to talk with a mouth full of food.

The farmer and his wife each made a show of taking big bites of their cakes and chewing easily. The kelpie did the same.

"You see, these special griddle cakes are no problem for our entire family, even those of us that are wee," Brigid explained.

She took another whopping bite out of the griddle cake and chewed as the giant leaned down and watched closely.

"Why does it not break your teeth?" he asked.

Brigid finished chewing, swallowed and then told him, "My teeth are fine. And the griddle cakes are delicious!"

Brigid then picked up the plate of griddle cakes and held it up toward the giant. "Maybe," she explained, "you will do better with some from the second batch. Go ahead. Try again. Or are you too weak to eat what my father eats?"

With that, the farmer and his wife took another bite from their griddle cakes and chewed noisily.

"Give me that!" the giant growled as he took six griddle cakes from the stack on the plate in Brigid's outstretched hands.

They all watched as the giant shoved the stack into his mouth and bit down hard.

Crack!

And another tooth fell from the giant's mouth.

"Ouchy, ouchy, ouch!" he cried.

"I don't understand your problem," Brigid said as she took another bite from a griddle cake.

"Your father eaths those griddle cakths every day?" lisped the giant. Some of his words sounded very peculiar because of his missing two front teeth, but nobody dared laugh at that moment.

"Of course, he does!" exclaimed Brigid.

"You're a family tough ath oak treeth. H-how big ith thish father of yourth?"

"He's so big," Brigid explained, "that to make sure we have a sunshiny morn, he reaches up and taps the sun itself ahead of him on his way from the other side of the world."

As luck would have it, a small cloud passed in front of the sun causing the day to darken and then lighten again.

"There he is now!" Brigid shouted.

"He ith?" asked the giant in a very timid voice and looking too afraid to actually turn around and have a look.

"Isn't that the very top of his head I see?" the

kelpie remarked shading his eyes with his hooves.

"Mornin', Dad!" Brigid shouted. "Your griddle cakes be on the griddle!" Then turning to the farmer and his wife she ordered, "Get more griddle cakes in the pans! Dad will be here very soon!"

"Yes, dear!" the farmer's wife replied and she began waving at the unseen giant of giants.

"What's she doing now?" the farmer asked his wife.

"Waving to her Dad, the giant of giants, who's bringing the sun with him to breakfast. Wave, man, wave with us!"

"She's nothing but daft," the famer uttered as he waved in the same direction as Brigid and his wife.

"She's nothing but life-saving smart," his wife corrected him, "that's what she is. Wave to her father!"

"Top 'o the morning sir!" the kelpie shouted.

For fear of what he might see, the giant still didn't even turn around to look in the direction they were waving.

"Maybe I should be leaving," the giant observed.

"It's not a good thing to be dith-turbing a fellow gianth's morning meal. Tho long!" And he hurried away.

The ground shook with every leap.

"There's breakfast every morning," Brigid shouted after him.

"You're welcome to come back," the kelpie called out.

"No thank you!" he shouted back over his shoulder. "I am never ever coming thith way ever, ever again!"

They all watched as the giant ran across the farmer's pasture, across the next pasture, and up a broad hill. They felt the ground shake less and less as the giant disappeared from sight.

In relief, the farmer's wife and Brigid fell to the ground laughing.

"I'll be eating what's left of my breakfast then," the farmer exclaimed grabbing the plate of cakes and beginning to eat.

The kelpie quickly took the second stack and began savoring them one by one.

"Thanks, me darlin' girl!" cried the farmer's wife when their laughter diminished.

"How did I do that?" Brigid uttered in amazement.

"With my griddle cakes, his iron horse shoes and your amazing gift for blarney my dear child. That is how."

"I am so sorry your barn is in ruins!" Brigid exclaimed.

"But our lives are not, thanks to you."

"She's daft," the farmer exclaimed between bites, "but clever, too."

"Smartness it took to fool a foolish giant," the farmer's wife declared and gave Brigid a hug. "Frightened by the tale you told, he'll not ever return. Don't you be ungrateful Liam, dear! Thank her!"

"Thank you, lass," said the farmer. "You are, for certain, a clever one at that!"

"That she is. That she is," his wife added beaming the biggest of smiles. "You will stay and have more breakfast with us, will you not?"

"Thank you, ma'am. The cake I ate was plenty. I must say farewell and be on my way."

"Then a safe journey to you, my dear," she said kissing Brigid on the forehead.

The farmer's wife gathered up her plate and pan, the farmer gathered up the giant's teeth, one under each arm.

"God's speed, little one," the farmer added.

Brigid and the kelpie watched as the farmer and his wife returned to their little farmhouse and closed the door behind them.

Brigid and the kelpie were alone.

"We've become quite a frightful team, kelpie."

"It was you who did it," the kelpie assured her.

But she brushed off his words. She either didn't hear or she pretended not to hear his flattering words. She withdrew the Bard's Rod from her belt and began to chant, "Tap once twice, thrice. Bard's Rod, point ..."

"Ahem!" uttered the kelpie, interrupting her chant. "It's you who will be going."

"No. Us. Together."

"No. You. I will be waiting here for new shoes." He hopped gingerly on his shoeless hind legs. "Ooh, ouch, pretty pretty feet, delicate and tender, ooh, ouch!"

"But I cannot face another challenge without you, Kelpie!" she lamented.

"I suppose that's true enough. You'd not have smartly fooled that giant without my standing beside you as an intimidating warning to the brute."

"You!" Brigid exclaimed, "You did nothing!"

"Are you telling me, then, you did it all? Defeated the giant all by yourself?"

Brigid thought for a moment. A big smile came across her face and she admitted, "Well I did now, didn't I?"

"Yes, you did," the kelpie affirmed. "Not bad for a human," he added with a wink and a crooked smile.

Brigid moved to him and gave the kelpie a quick hug around the neck. "Thank you. That is high praise coming from a creature like you."

A sudden breeze began to blow and a billowing cloud of water vapor was soon upon them. Before they could move in any direction they were surrounded by the sprites and tiny glowing creatures Brigid had seen once before at the Cliffs of Moher.

"Oh my!" she exclaimed.

"We have visitors from the sea! Hurrah!" exclaimed the kelpie.

The mist swirled and swirled and then a portion of it began to take shape. A moment later, standing there before them was the beautiful Sea Mither.

"So," Brigid asked "what shall be the second test of the three you told me?"

"But it is already two tests that you've now passed," the Sea Mither explained approvingly.

"What?!"

"I was the first test," admitted the kelpie.

"You?"

"A test of your heart," the Sea Mither confirmed.

"I was purposely nasty. I threatened your very life."

"You could have been killed by the rising tides," Brigid protested.

"So, you untied me, didn't you?" added the kelpie.

"You saved his life, Brigid," Sea Mither affirmed,

"even after he had threatened yours. It was a true test of the heart."

"And you befriended me along the way," the kelpie added.

"If the kelpie was my first test, then the Giant was the second test for certain, was it not?" Brigid asked.

"A true test of your mind," said the Sea Mither.

"I always knew you were very intelligent and very clever," the kelpie teased her.

"But now," Brigid started to speak.

"Now a third and final test awaits you, Brigid Shawn O'Grady."

"But Sea Mither, dear Sea Mither, must I go alone? A test all by myself? It's too hard. I am frightened to go alone."

"Which is the purpose of the test, my dear. The third is a test of courage."

"Go, Brigid," the kelpie urged. "Go and you'll have that wish of yours answered!"

"I do not want to say goodbye to you." Brigid explained as she reached out and stroked the kelpie's golden mane. "So, I will just go." And she turned away from him and faced the Sea Mither.

"Trust the Bard's Rod," the Sea Mither reminded her. "Follow it without a swerve or curve and you will find your way to the Sage at the well at the world's edge."

"Thank you, ma'am, thank you!"

With that, the sprites, the glowing little creatures and the mist began to swirl around the Sea Mither and the kelpie. The mist grew thicker and swirled faster and faster until the cloud of vapor rose up, moved towards the sea and out of sight.

Brigid took the Bard's Rod in both hands and tapped the earth as she recited, "Tap once, twice, thrice. Bard's Rod point the way to the well at world's edge. Point the way to what I need. Point the way!"

And off she went in the direction it led.

CHAPTER FIVE
The Bog Serpent

So there she was, a little girl in a land of talking animals, giants, flying fairies and many other wondrous creatures.

Brigid walked, and walked and walked. As she did, it seemed that every creature, even the flowers and the trees, were watching her.

The wonder and strangeness enchanted her. She wasn't afraid for her safety but one thing did concern her a great deal.

Everyone here sees my foot, and the difference, and the ugliness. But in this world, no one cares! She thought to herself.

Four pixies sitting on a large flower blossom saw Brigid as she approached. They left their perch and flew over and around Brigid as she was walking along.

"Hello?" Brigid said with uncertainty. She wasn't sure if they spoke the same language. But she soon learned that they did because without even saying hello back, the four creatures began chattering amongst themselves.

"She's got no wings, no feathers."

"'Tis one of those humans."

"No scales, no fins."

"No stripes on her, no spots of any kind."

"Just like a human."

"No fur, no tail."

"So big compared to us."

"But small compared to a dragon."

Brigid stopped walking. The pixies hovered all around her.

"Dragon? Where is there a dragon?" she asked the wee flying pixies.

"Oh, don't let her frighten you," a pixie assured Brigid. "There are no dragons anymore."

"They only live in stories," another pixie added.

"I like the stories!" the third pixie cried. "Do not make fun of the stories."

"I don't think she's making fun of you," Brigid explained to the pouting pixie. "Besides, dragons can be exciting! In stories anyway. Don't you think?"

"Yes, yes, yes!"

"Well, Rose Petal, it seems you have found a friend."

"Maybe we all have!"

"My name is Brigid," she announced and began walking again.

The four pixies then introduced themselves as Ivy, Rose Petal, Moonlight and Wintergreen. Since they all looked very similar, Brigid could not easily tell them apart. *They talk so fast,* Brigid thought to herself.

"The whole forest has been watching out for you."

"How would you know about me?" Brigid asked as she continued walking.

"A sooty tern from the far away sea. Well, he didn't exactly tell us directly."

"He told a falcon who told a pine marten who told just about everyone he has encountered since."

"Pine martens are very curious creatures."

"Downright nosey and into everything."

"And they love to chatter about whatever they see and hear and they will talk to everyone."

"And that," asked Brigid, "is not just in stories?"

"No, he is for real."

"As real at that Bard's Rod you carry."

"As real as your journey."

"And as real as your quest to reach the old woman at the well at the world's edge."

"But why do you want to go all that way?"

"I have a wish to make," Brigid shyly explained.

"She has a wish to make!"

"Ooooh, I love wishes!"

"A wish for what?"

"Tell us, please tell us!"

"This foot of mine," Brigid explained, holding out her large boot-covered foot.

"Foot?"

"What about it?"

"Don't you see," asked Brigid as she raised her skirt slightly. "This misshaped foot is very different from my other one."

"So, what if they are different?"

"That's not the way they're supposed to be?"

"Why does it even matter?"

"That's hardly strange at all."

"Is it more strange than jumping off a very tall cliff into the sea?"

"More strange than a friendly helpful kelpie?"

"Or a giant?"

"How do you know all of that?"

"A chatty sooty tern …"

"… and a talkative falcon."

"… and a pine marten who tells everyone everything. How else?"

Brigid let her dress down over her foot and looked back at the pixies without a word. *I thought that they would see my foot and the difference and the ugliness. But in this world no one does.*

"Rest a while with us in our land."

"Take a bite or two of this," said Moonlight as she handed Brigid a square of yellow cake.

"You can stay as long as you wish!"

"We can share stories!"

"This is delicious!" Brigid said, "Thank you! You

are all so kind, but I must keep going forward."

They continued to keep Brigid company, chattering away about this and that and so quickly that Brigid was never quite sure which pixie was which or what they were chattering about. But she appreciated the company all the same.

As evening approached, Brigid started hearing some strange sounds up ahead. She walked faster and faster and as she did, the sounds grew more distinct. They were sounds of frogs and water fowl and crickets that were punctuated now and then by a splash.

Brigid hurried up a small rise and then stopped. Stretching out in front of her from her toes to the horizon was a dark, wet and seemingly endless bog.

She took the rod from her belt and tapped the earth as she recited, "Tap once, twice, thrice. Bard's Rod, point the way to the well at world's edge. Point the way to what I need. Point the way!"

Brigid twirled and stopped. The rod pointed straight out across foreboding bog.

"What does that mean? What does that mean?" she

heard a little's boy's voice ask.

Brigid turned and saw a pine marten standing nearby, its thick brown fur coat and its yellow fur bib catching the rays of the setting sun. He had a look of wonder about him.

"'Tis pointing straight ahead, surely to the well at the world's edge," Brigid explained. "But without a curve or a swerve through that muck and mud?"

A stately and very dignified heron slowly approached. The pine marten ran to him.

"See? There she is, there she is!" the pine marten explained to the heron. "I told you she was coming!"

"You have told everyone, Marty," Wintergreen remarked.

The pixies settled on a moss-covered log nearby.

No one spoke a word. They just watched Brigid staring out across the immense bog.

She finally broke the silence. "Oh my," she sighed.

"There is no way 'round," the Heron informed her in a dignified voice.

Brigid thought, *first a pine marten and now a*

heron saying words to me? Another talking animal? She smiled. *Whoever would have guessed it would become so normal? 'Tis a world of wonders! It's all like pages lifted from my book of tales.*

"When human children come here ..." the heron began.

"They all think," Marty interrupted, "'this is strange. 'Tis mighty strange.'"

"Aye, that they do," confirmed the heron.

"Others have been here before me?" Brigid asked.

"Children only," the heron assured her.

"They've been here." Marty further explained, "to this spot, but no further. Not a one got past."

"And across this bog is the only way to the well at world's edge," the heron reminded her.

"The only way?" Brigid asked.

"Our young pine marten is correct," the heron answered. "You must go forward or go back. There is, in this situation, no this side or that ... only straight ahead or back."

"Then this is my third test. I must make it past the

slime and stink of that moss and mud."

"Mud, mud, ooh, I love mud!" Marty sang out. "Mud is for jumping and diving, swimming and frolicking and splishing and splashing!" With a splat the pine marten dove into the bog. He quickly resurfaced cooing, "Mud, mud, ooh, I love the slick and the slimy muck of the wonderful mud!"

"Not only must you make it past the muck and mud as you call it, dear Brigid, but there's the serpent as well."

"Serpent?" asked Brigid.

"Not just in the stories," Rose Pedal sadly assured her.

"As real as the giant," affirmed Wintergreen.

"Ack! The serpent!" Marty shrieked and jumped out of the bog. "The serpent is no fun at all."

"It is a terrible and mighty fierce serpent," explained the heron.

"An ugly serpent who likes to eat pine martens for breakfast. Evil. Evil through and through. Evil and ugly from his wicked face to the tip of his pointed tail! So ugly!"

"Marty!" the heron interrupted him. "She understands that point, I am sure."

"I believe I do," Brigid responded in almost a whisper.

"Many others have been here before you, Brigid," the heron went on to explain. "And almost every child has run away in fright. Then there was that last one. She stood right there, frozen in fear."

"She was the Bog Serpent's lunch," Marty added and shivered.

"So, it is the Bog Serpent you must face, the heron continued. "He guards this place and the well at world's edge that is beyond the great bog before you."

"I have no weapons! How do I defeat a serpent with just my hands and a stick?"

The pixies spoke up.

"You can use your head!"

"And your cunning!"

"And your courage!"

"You can do it!" they cheered and then they applauded loudly.

The heron cleared his throat loudly and the pixies quieted down. "It has been told that the tongue will tame him," the heron explained.

"The tongue will tame him?" Brigid asked.

"Oh surely, lots o'luck," said Marty. "The tongue that's in his mouth must be grabbed."

"I must grab its tongue?"

"Yes, by reaching past his terrible poisonous fangs," the heron confirmed.

Suddenly the pixies shrieked. The others turned and saw why. A large, ugly bog serpent rose out of the muck a ways away, looked in their direction, and then it dove back down into the bog.

"I cannot!" cried Brigid.

"Then be gone and that's the end of it," the heron stated matter-of-factly.

"Oh, but it does look large and terrible," Brigid fretted. "But the Sage is beyond the bog. How will I do this?"

Leading her to a large round and dirty stone at the edge of the bog, Marty the pine marten explained, "You need to stand on this, the Serpent's Rock."

"It looks to have only room for normal feet!" Brigid exclaimed.

"You must stand here upon this rock."

"I cannot with this weak and twisted foot of mine," she fretted.

The heron bent over, examined Brigid's misshaped foot closely then stood erect. "Does it not make the other foot stronger?" he asked.

"I never thought about it that way," she marveled and then stepped up on the serpent's rock commenting, "Such a small rock and slippery besides."

The Heron tilted his head, studied Brigid and then asked, "Are your <u>thoughts</u> small? Do your <u>feelings</u> slip and slide?"

"Right now, my feelings are pretty steady."

"That's good! Stand still!" Marty instructed. "Stand very still."

"He's a touchy sort of monster, that one is," said the heron.

"Very moody," Marty agreed.

106

As Brigid tried one position then another for her feet, and tried to stand very still, the heron and the pine marten continued to offer instructions and warnings.

"Any movement …"

"A twitch or an itch."

"… will defeat you. And you must be very quiet. The smallest of sounds …"

"… like a moan or a groan."

"And – quick – he'll sting you into frozen submission!"

"... and then eat you whole!"

Brigid had become very still. She didn't mean to be impolite, but she stopped listening and simply concentrated on her breathing. Then she quietly announced, "I can be still. I can be quiet." And she added, "The tongue will tame him." Then she didn't move another muscle.

Suddenly the bog serpent's head rose from the muck of the bog. More of his long scaly body could be seen as he rose higher and higher into the air. Then he quickly sank back into the muck and was gone.

"This, I remember," the Heron announced, "is when that wee girl with red hair ran away shrieking."

The bog serpent suddenly reappeared closer still. It bared its terrible poisonous fangs and hissed loudly.

"This is when that tall and mighty boy shivered, eyes wide, he jumped off the rock and crawled away crying."

The bog serpent rose higher still and came face to face with Brigid.

"And this," the Heron whispered. "is where nobody moves."

The heron, the pine marten and the pixies kept very, very still with their eyes glued on Brigid and the bog serpent.

Brigid stood so very still that she did not even blink as the bog serpent began to coil around her body

"Tis foolish you are, and ugly and weak," the serpent hissed.

It curled over the backs of her legs and slid around like a slick and slimy belt at her waist repeating, "'Tis foolish you are, and ugly and weak."

Yet Brigid moved not at all.

It slithered up and over her shoulders, insisting ever louder this time, "'Tis foolish you are, and ugly and weak!"

Then, with its head raised high, it stared down at her. It emitted an awful hiss. Its lips curled back revealing sharp yellow fangs. It was as if time had stopped and everything was very still for a moment. Then the vile serpent slowly opened his mouth very wide to make a meal of her. His tongue was wagging in anticipation.

But …

Quick and strong and straight, Brigid reached up with both hands and grabbed the serpent's tongue! With more vigor than she ever imagined she had, she held on to the tongue as the huge bog serpent struggled against captivity. It flopped up and down and sideways in its attempt to free itself, but Brigid was unshaken. It was as if, by holding the tongue, she had all the strength in the world and her body was straight and strong as a marble statue.

For what seemed like the longest time ever, the bog serpent jerked and writhed but it could not escape her grasp. Finally, it flopped down on the reedy edge of the bog one last time and, like Brigid, it became motionless. Even then, she did not let go of its tongue. She didn't dare.

For a moment there was complete silence. It was as if every creature in or near the bog was holding its breath.

Suddenly the heron and the pine marten shouted out, "Hazzah!"

The pixies applauded and shrieked their approval.

"She's done it!" declared the heron.

"No one's ever done what she has done! She's tamed the serpent!" cried the pine marten.

Without moving a muscle or blinking an eye, Brigid calmly asked those watching, "What is next?"

"What? What? What's next? What's next?" chattered the pixies.

"Legend has it," the heron explained, "that you," he paused to clear his throat then continued, "you let go of the serpent's tongue."

Brigid turned her head and stared at the heron in

disbelief.

"Let ... go ... of its tongue?" Brigid asked over her shoulder. "Rose Petal is that in any of the stories?"

"None I have read," Rose Pedal replied.

"Perhaps it is true, then," said Brigid who paused a moment and then let go of the serpent's tongue.

Nobody breathed.

Everything stayed very still.

The serpent didn't move.

"Oh my!" Brigid shouted. "N-Now what?!" Brigid studied the very still serpent. She looked over the vast bog and then at the creatures around her. With great smiles of affection, they chanted:

"Now, you know in your brain ..."

"Now, you know in your heart ..."

"Now you know in your skin and your bones ... "

"That you will not ever be the same."

"That "Brigid" will forevermore mean "strength.""

"That 'Shawn' will forevermore mean "one-of-a-kind.""

"Brigid Shawn O'Grady," the heron explained,

"you know <u>now</u> what you are destined to do."

"I do!" Brigid shouted.

"What?" asked Marty. "What?"

"This!" Brigid declared and she grabbed one of the horns atop the serpent's head and she swung around and up on to the serpent's back. She took the Bard's Rod from her belt and raised it high above her head.

"Chin on the ground!" she commanded.

The serpent rested its chin on the earth. Brigid leaned over and struck the ground three times as she chanted, "Tap once, twice, thrice! Bard's Rod, point the way to the well at world's edge. Point the way to what I need. Point the way."

She settled back and held tightly to one of the serpent's horns. The rod once again pointed straight out over the bog. Brigid turned to her friends and declared, "Thank you my wonderful friends! Now onward!"

The bog serpent rose off the ground and flew out over the bog taking a triumphant Brigid Shawn O'Grady with him.

She replaced the Bard's Rod in her belt and held on

to both of the serpent's horns as it flew high into pillow-like, puffy clouds. The sunlight and the air felt warm upon her face as they flew towards a wonderfully colorful sunset. A wind caused her hair to trail so straight out behind that she wondered if any curls would be left at the end of their flight. This made her laugh out loud. She was not scared, she was not amazed. She enjoyed the flight so much that she let go of the horns and leaned over and hugged the serpent with all the warmth and affection she could muster.

"Thank you, thank you!" she shouted to be heard against the wind.

Suddenly there came a strange sound. A popping kind of sound started and continued as the serpent's ugly brown and green scales changed color one after another after another. Before long, Brigid was riding atop a far more benign looking serpent with smooth shiney yellow scales.

Days ago, when she was riding the galloping kelpie she had imagined she was flying. Now there was no imagination needed. She was soaring through the air with heightened senses. Never before had she so clearly felt the strength of the wind and the power of magic. She had always believed magic to be good and today she was more certain than ever.

Brigid hugged the serpent again and held on tight as they flew down out of the clouds. She could see the bog was far beyond them and that the ground was coming closer. The serpent flew lower, gently sliding to a stop on a dirt plain surround by tall mountains.

Brigid slid down the side of the beast and walked towards the small pool of crystal clear water nearby.

Standing next to the water was a figure whose face was concealed by the hood of her emerald green robe.

CHAPTER SIX
The Well At The World's Edge

"You! You're the Sage!"

"Yes, I am the Sage you seek." She removed the hood of her cloak revealing a gentle loving face of an elderly women framed by blonde hair. Her blue eyes sparkled as she crooned, "Welcome, Brigid Shawn O'Grady."

"You know my name?"

"And your destiny."

"To change this misshapen foot of mine to be like my other, and like everyone else's. I have passed the test of three."

"Yes. With an act of kindness for the kelpie, which was a test of your heart.

"And then, I defeated the giant."

"Very clever. A test of how smart you truly are."

"And now, taming the deadly bog serpent."

"Indeed you did, passing the test of courage."

"So. Here I am at last. The Sea Mither promised

that you could rid me of this ugly misshapen foot."

"Are you sure that's what you want?"

"Am I sure? Am I sure I want to be normal?"

"I ask you to ask yourself."

Brigid considered that for a moment and then she spoke. "Well. You know, no one noticed my foot amongst all the giants and mermaids and talking animals. And I did befriend the kelpie, and I did outsmart a giant, and tamed the bog serpent."

"And that misshaped foot of yours?" asked the Sage.

"This foot? My misshaped foot?" Brigid did not answer immediately. She took a moment for remembering. *When I rescued the kelpie, when I was tricking the giant, and even when I was face to face with that bog serpent ... all those times ... I never thought one moment about this foot.*

"And that foot of yours?" the Sage asked again.

"It had nothing to do with it."

"Ah, a promise kept. I need only show you to yourself." The Sage led Brigid to the crystal-clear pool of water, explaining, "The magic of this well is in the mirror made of its water. 'Tis a mirror showing you as you see yourself. Look now, at how you saw yourself before your journey."

Brigid studied her reflection in the pool of water.

"That's me? I see a very large and ugly foot. 'Tis almost all of me."

The Sage waved her hand over the water and told Brigid, "Look you here again. How do you see yourself now?"

Staring down at the well, Brigid saw herself. She smiled back at herself.

"Do you see a kind and smart and brave person?"

"Yes, I do," replied Brigid.

"And your foot?" asked the Sage.

"That foot, is only one part of who I am. And not the most important part. There is no need to change it."

"Ah, a promise kept." The Sage concurred. "The magic has happened."

"It has. It has! Thank you!"

Once again Brigid felt a familiar warm breeze and

117

enjoyed the aroma of salty ocean air. She turned and saw a billowing cloud of misty water vapor flying toward them.

"My friends from the sea!"

The mist swirled and swirled and then became still. It dissolved enough to reveal the many sea creatures and the beautiful Sea Mither who walked to Brigid and the Sage.

"Well done, Brigid," said the Sea Mither in as welcomed and beautiful a voice as anyone ever heard.

"You are the first child ever to reach me and this well," the Sage explained. "You have done a great thing, and we offer you our praise. Stay with us. And your difference will be no difference at all. You'll feast upon cakes and drink sweet nectar."

"Stay here, if you'd like," the Sea Mither added. "Stay here with all the wonderful folk you have met. Play with the animals of our magical forests and seas."

"Here you close your eyes and dream tales of wonder and beauty. Here the unknown can be proven good."

Brigid closed her eyes and imagined much of what

the Sage and the Sea Mither had just described.

"'Tis your choice to make, dear Brigid," the Sage explained.

Brigid sighed. "It is all so wonderful." She took a deep breath and opened her eyes. Present now were all of her new friends: the kelpie, the heron, the pine marten and the four pixies.

"Oh my," she cried as she looked from one to another of her friends. "But there is my mother and father, and the rivers and the hills of my County Clare."

"Close your eyes one more time," the Sea Mither suggested.

Brigid closed her eyes.

"Can you remember from where you came?" the Sea Mither asked. "Can you see the village where some will never understand that different is not scary? That different is just different?"

"See a village where they scorn you and mock you," The Sage added. "See a village where someone unlike everyone else is seen as something less. For them, different is frightful, hateful or evil."

Brigid opened her eyes and looked at her friends and felt their love.

The four pixies flew up to her as they chattered away:

"Oh my, you humans!"

"You can make what is small seem so very big!"

"You can make the big – your hearts and minds …"

"… seem as almost nothing at all."

Brigid thought for a moment, then with certainty she announced, "I'll be going home."

"Brigid Shawn O'Grady," the Sage gently explained, "take the rod again and tap three times. You will find yourself wherever you wish."

Brigid look a moment to look around.

"Fare thee well, young lady," said the heron.

The pine martin hopped up into Brigid's arms. She hugged him. "Thanks to you I can swim in all the mud I want! Bye-bye!" He hugged her and he jumped away.

The kelpie danced over to her and announced, "Need a hero, need a friend, call on me!"

The Sea Mither leaned over and kissed Brigid on the forehead. "You will now be brave forever."

The Sage did the same, and told Brigid, "... and wise forever as well. Tell of this journey of yours and the grown-ups in your life will not believe you. But the children will."

"Thank you," Brigid told them and smiled a very broad smile.

"And you ..." she began as she walked over to the serpent which had curled up at the Sea Mither's feet. "You really are quite beautiful." She reached out and stroked its smooth yellow fur. It turned its head and Brigid looked deep into the bog serpent's emerald green eyes. "I will never forget our flight together," she told him and gave him a hug.

She then ran over to the kelpie and hoped upon his back shouting, "I wish I could take you with me!" And she leaned over and hugged his neck and then stroked his golden mane. "Oh, kelpie, what tales we both now have to tell. We'll never again eat griddle cakes and not think of each other!"

"For ever and ever," the kelpie told her and then knelt forward for her to slide off his back.

Standing there, Brigid sighed.

She took a look moment for a last look at all of her new friends. She then stepped away from them all, tapped the rod to the earth three times and the world of wonders dissolved.

In an instant, she was at the door of her home. Brigid opened the door and walked into the empty cottage.

CHAPTER SEVEN
Home Again

Brigid went to the table and opened her book. She found her pen and ink that she used to practice her letters and numbers and she quickly wrote two short sentences inside the book's front cover. She left the book open on the table so the ink would dry and she replaced the pen and the ink well on the mantel above the fireplace.

She was standing by the fireplace when her mother came back inside carrying the bucket. Brigid ran to her and gave her a big hug. Never in her life had it felt so good to be close to her mother.

"Five minutes and I still see a clean broom and dirty floor?"

"Five ... minutes?" Brigid asked as she backed away. "But it has been days. It was almost a week ago I untied the kelpie. We defeated the giant and then it was days before I rode the serpent to the well at the world's edge."

"Ah, you have been wasting time day-dreaming!"

"No. It was real!" Brigid exclaimed and she went to the table to get the book to show her mother what she had written.

But before she could pick up the book her father entered the cottage to retrieve the hat he had forgotten. He turned to Brigid. "You are to get rid of that book! I will not tell you again. 'Tis a world of fantasy and lies!"

"No, Father. 'Tis a world of my possibilities. I'll be going to school, Mother. I need the learning, like everyone else. I need more than fairy tales. I'm ready for that now, Father and you must let me go."

"I'll not abide those village folk mistreating my only daughter because of that misshaped foot of yours."

"Then it is their problem. I'll not make it mine. The foot is only one part of who I am, it is not all of me. There are other parts and they are brave, and clever and kind. I know that now for certain, Father. I'll not be 'little' any longer."

"A father must protect his child from the harsh world's harm."

"You do. I carry your caring with me, Father. 'Tis

here," she said, indicating her heart. "And here," she added, indicating her head.

At that, her father stepped aside, watching closely as Brigid walked out of the house and up the road to the village.

Standing by the table, her mother noticed the Bard's Rod. She picked it up and examined the carving. "Ta' draichot anseo. Ta' aochas anseo," she read. "What is this? Have you seen this?" She asked her husband.

He took the rod and looked at it closely. "Ta' draichot anseo. Ta' aochas anseo. It is Gaelic. Magic is here. Hope is here. Where did our child get a Bard's Rod?"

Her mother looked at the opened book on the table and read, "'From this day forward Brigid will forever mean strength. Shawn will forever mean one-of-a-kind.' And 'tis signed 'Brigid Shawn O'Grady.' Well, husband, how about that?"

They looked at each other a moment and then quickly left the cottage and hurried toward the village.

As the approached they saw their daughter walk to the school building. Several townspeople stood in her way.

125

"You do not belong here," insisted the street sweeper.

"Not pretty at all," a woman complained to her companion.

"Twisted inside and out," she responded.

"A mistake," insisted a farmer.

"A monster," said another.

Brigid's father pushed his way past the townspeople surrounding his daughter, asking, "Do we have a problem here?"

Brigid looked up. "There is no problem now, Father," she insisted with certainty.

Without a word of reproach, he handed her the Bard's Rod.

Brigid smiled and slipped it into her belt.

The school door opened and the teacher stood blocking Brigid's way. "This, Michael Sean O'Grady, is a very poor choice."

"I think not," he replied.

Suddenly the little girl snuck past the teacher and walked up to Brigid. "Hi. You came back! Remember me?

My name's Brianna. What's yours?" She held out her hand. Brigid took it.

"My name is Brigid Shawn O'Grady and I am here for school and learning."

"But," the teacher started saying, "the frightful difference …"

"Oh that?" said Brigid very loudly and in a very dismissive tone. "I believe it is a misshaped foot. My foot is just one small part of me, ma'am. Would you like to get to know the rest and the best of me?"

This put quite a look of surprise on the teacher's face. She did not know what to say. So, she stepped aside.

Brigid and Brianna walked into the school together as the teacher looked to Michael O'Grady. He simply shrugged his shoulders and smiled broadly.

The villagers looked to one another silently. In light of the child's courageous announcement, there was nothing else to be said.

The teacher returned to her pupils and the townspeople went their ways.

Mr. and Mrs. O'Grady held hands walking home

that morning, and they talked happily of the days yet to come.

For years, Brigid's own children and her childrens' children would pick up the Bard's Rod and feel the magic of it. When they asked, they would be told the story – this story - of its origin.

The O'Grady family would long remember how it pointed the way to possibilities, to hopes and to dreams for Brigid Shawn O'Grady in long ago County Clare, Ireland.

Made in the USA
Columbia, SC
22 March 2018